The LITTLE HEN and the GREAT WAR

Thi

Th
a f

The Trenches, 1917

Bertha, aged 8, 1916

OF THE "WILLOCHRA" IN WELLINGTON HARBOUR

Photo, Henris Sarony

Arthur Brewer

RETURN OF TROOPSHIP

Artist's models—
Kelly Isabella and Bessie

OVER THERE

WHANGAHOMONA.

First published in 1996 by Scholastic New Zealand Limited as *The Bantam and the Soldier*
First published in the UK in 2014 by Scholastic Children's Books
Euston House, Eversholt Street, London NW1 1DB
a division of Scholastic Ltd
www.scholastic.co.uk
London ~ New York ~ Toronto ~ Sydney ~ Auckland
Mexico City ~ New Delhi ~ Hong Kong

Text copyright © 1996 Jennifer Beck
Illustrations copyright © 1996 Robyn Belton

ISBN 978 1407 14598 3

Printed in Singapore

1 3 5 7 9 10 8 6 4 2

The moral rights of Jennifer Beck and Robyn Belton have been asserted.

Redesign by Book Design Ltd, www.BookDesign.co.nz
Typeset in Bembo 15/23

Papers used by Scholastic Children's Books are made from wood grown in sustainable forests

The LITTLE HEN and the GREAT WAR

Jennifer Beck · Robyn Belton

SCHOLASTIC

ON THE OUTSKIRTS of a village in France, an elderly farmer kept a flock of bantam hens in his barn. Among them was one little hen who was sometimes pecked by the others. Food was scarce, and they would not always let her share the grain the farmer threw them.

It was wartime. The old stone barn echoed to the sounds of heavy tanks rolling past, and to the beat of soldiers' boots as regiment after regiment marched towards the battlefield just over the hill.

The rattle of machine-gun fire and the flash of shells exploding in the distance had been part of the hen's life from the beginning. She had grown used to the sounds of war. She was more afraid of the sharp beaks and claws of some of her barnyard companions.

The battle spread towards the village. When the smell of gunpowder began to drift across the farmyard, the farmer herded together his best animals and prepared to drive them to safer land further south. As he did not have enough room for the hens, the farmer opened the barn door and left them to fend for themselves.

The hens scratched about in the farmyard during the day, and returned to the barn to roost in the evening. That is, all except the smallest hen. She kept apart from the others, foraging in nearby fields and sleeping at night under an overgrown hedge by the roadside.

One night there was a deafening explosion. A stray shell had landed near the farmyard. The barn collapsed into a heap of broken beams and jumbled stones.

Then there was silence. Only the hen under the hedge survived, but in the blast she was thrown among the branches and could not struggle free.

It so happened that the very next morning a company of soldiers marched through the village towards the battlefield. They had come from a country on the other side of the world to join their allies. In those days they called it the Great War, and believed it was the war that would end all wars.

The soldiers had been marching for many hours. There were sighs of relief when they were allowed to rest for a while by the roadside.

One of the youngest among them was a farmer's son called Arthur. He loved farm life, and until a year before had travelled no further than a hundred miles from home. In war-torn Europe he often felt homesick and afraid, but tried not to show it. The older soldiers teased him enough as it was for his shyness and quiet country ways.

Sitting slightly apart from the others, Arthur took out a postcard to send to his family back home. He was thinking about his young niece, who liked to visit the farm during the school holidays. Arthur had just written 'Give my love to Bertha,' when he saw a movement in the hedge. It was the hen, trapped between branches and by then too weak to make a sound.

"Take it easy, little one," Arthur whispered as he cradled the quivering bird in his hands and eased her gently through the tangle of thorns.

Just then the officer in charge shouted, "Time's up, men!" and the soldiers struggled reluctantly to their feet and began to line up on the road.

"Hurry up there!" the officer ordered, when he noticed Arthur standing facing the hedge. What was Arthur to do? Hastily, he unbuttoned his thick khaki uniform and slipped the little hen inside his jacket.

That evening, Arthur fed the hen some food
he had saved. The other soldiers shook their
heads and laughed at him.

"What's the use of keeping that miserable
looking bird?" one of them demanded.
"It's so scrawny, it wouldn't even
make a decent bowl of soup!"

"If it starts crowing in the night, I'll wring its skinny neck!" warned another.

"Her name is Bertha," replied Arthur, "and she needs someone to look after her."

At first, life in the trenches was not so bad. Arthur was able to share his food with Bertha, and she grew stronger. The soldiers stopped teasing Arthur, and began to look upon Bertha as a lucky mascot. They even helped him build a pen for her.

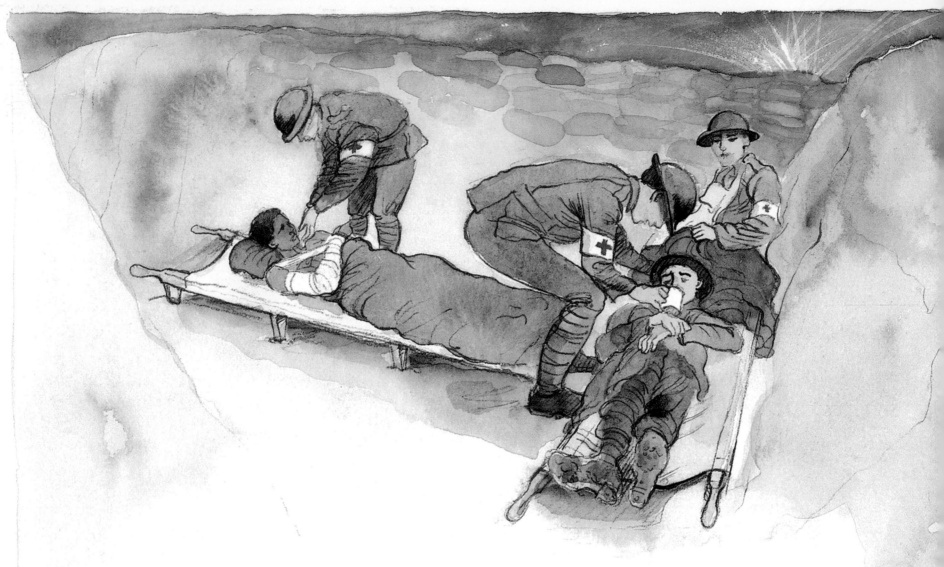

But the fighting grew heavier. Food became scarce, and Arthur and his companions collected grubs and worms for Bertha from the muddy banks of their clay prison.

And she rewarded them. In the midst of a raging battle, when the sky was crisscrossed with fire, Bertha laid a warm brown egg. When Arthur found it, he hugged the little hen to his mud-caked jacket.

Every morning from then on, as regular as daybreak, Bertha laid an egg for Arthur and his friends. They shared the eggs, a treat for those who were most in need. During the terrible weeks that followed, the hen gave them something to joke about. "A hen in the trench is worth five on the farm," they'd say, or "An egg a day keeps the shell shock away."

Above all, Bertha gave the soldiers courage and hope. "If a hen can live through this, and lay eggs as well," they told one another, "then perhaps we can survive this terrible war."

At last the battle front moved north, and the fighting began to draw to an end. Arthur and his remaining companions were able to clamber out of the waterlogged trenches and make their way back towards the camp across the mile or so of territory they had won.

When the soldiers had begun to recover their strength and it was time to leave, they pleaded to be allowed to take Bertha home with them.

"Sorry," replied the officer, "we've a long way to go. You must leave her here."

A few days later, those who were left of Arthur's regiment
once again marched past the farmyard. The farmer had returned,
and was unloading his cart.

Bertha had grown, and was now able to look after herself.
Arthur lifted the little hen out from under his jacket, and each
of his comrades in turn said goodbye to her.

Arthur was last. He whispered, "Thank you, Bertha, may you now live in freedom and peace," and gently set her down among the poppies that grew in the field beside the hedge.

Many months later, the soldiers left Europe on a troopship for home.
When they finally sailed into the harbour, the wharf was crowded
with people waiting to welcome them. Arthur's family hardly
recognised the tall young soldier being farewelled by his friends.

Arthur returned to the farm, and once again his niece Bertha went to visit during the school holidays. A flock of hens now foraged in the yard. Arthur showed Bertha how to feed and care for them, and they soon followed her everywhere.

Arthur never talked much about the war, but one day he said to his niece, "I want to tell you a story . . .

". . . about a hen I called Bertha."

AUTHOR'S NOTE

This is a story of what might have been.

The message on the postcard is a copy of one written to my grandmother in Auckland in 1917. My mother, Bertha, was Arthur's niece. Arthur Brewer was, in fact, marching to his death at the time he wrote that postcard. He did not have the opportunity to write the letter he promised would follow. Killed in action five days later at Messines Ridge, on the border of France and Belgium, Arthur was buried there. His family received the postcard after he died.

The idea of the bantam hen in the trenches came from a war photograph I noticed when leafing through a heap of discarded books in the Howick Library. I bought the book, *Animals in War*, for 50 cents.

Robyn Belton and I have discussed family losses through wars suffered by the generations that included our grandparents and parents. Arthur has been given a country background in memory of Robyn's three uncles who did not return to farms in the Wanganui area after World War II, and the many farmers' sons listed on the war memorial monument in Waipu, my home town.

This story is dedicated to them all.

JENNIFER BECK

The Great War 1914-1918

Certificate of the Services in the New Zealand Expeditionary Forces

RECORD OF WAR SERVICE

Certificate of War Service

NZ

ANZAC

"The Australian and New Zealand troops have indeed proved themselves worthy sons of the Empire."

BRITONS

Fall-in!

"WANTS" YOU

JOIN YOUR COUNTRY'S ARMY!

GOD SAVE THE KING

GALLIPOLI SOUVENIR

Lt. Gen. Sir W.R. Birdwood "The Soul of Anzac"

BRAVO ANZACS!

RINGS THE WIDE WORLD WITH THE FAME
AND GLORY OF AUSTRALIA'S NAME,
VALIANT SONS OF BRITAIN TRUE.
OUR GREAT EMPIRE PRAISES YOU!
AND TO HISTORY SHALL GO DOWN
NEW ZEALAND'S LOYAL AND BRAVE RENOWN.
ZEAL IN EVERY NOBLE HEART
ANSWERING PLAYS A HERO'S PART
CLOSER BINDS OUR EMPIRE'S TRACKS
SONS OF BRITAIN – BRAVE ANZACS.

Gas mask for a dog. From a display in QE II Military Museum, Waiouru

Don't worry, I'll soon be back.

The New Zealand General Hospital, No. 2, Walton-on-Thames.

PERMANENT PASS TO ADMIT TWO VISITORS.

PERMANENT PASS to admit two visitors to see No. 12543.
(Rank) Cpl. (Name) Hugh A Anderson.
whilst in Hospital. Ward 7.

RULES RELATING TO THIS PASS.

1. One of these Passes is to be given to each patient on his admission.
2. The patient is responsible that it is sent to the relative or friend he wishes to see.
3. He must obtain the Pass from the visitor at the end of the interview if he wishes to transfer it to anyone else for the next visiting day, otherwise the visitor may retain the Pass.
4. Only two visitors to visit the patient at one time. Other visitors may have the use of the Pass the same day, but they must wait downstairs in the Main Hall.
5. Visitors will be allowed on the following days :—
   TUESDAYS, 2 to 5 p.m. & Saturdays
   THURSDAYS, 2 to 5 p.m.
   SUNDAYS, 2 to 5 p.m.
   Visitors will only be allowed at other times if the patient is on the danger list.
6. If this Pass is lost, a Patient cannot obtain a second Pass.
7. On discharge from hospital Patients must return their passes to the Sister of the Ward.

16 JUL 1917
No. 2 NEW ZEALAND GENERAL HOSPITAL
ON-ON-THAMES.

THE BEST OF ALL
LEMON SQUEEZERS.
WILL EXTRACT THE "Last Drop."
RETAIL 4½D. 4½D. EACH.
EASLEY'S PA
ALWAYS BRIGHT & CLEAN.

BRAVO!
AUSTRALIA & NEW ZEALAND.

Hugh Alexander Anderson

Ruby Eleanor Anderson

Original Postcard from Arthur dated June 2. 1917

CARTE POSTALE

Paris (Marque deposée)

June 2nd 1917

Dear Lib

Very sorry being unable to write for some time for we have been very busy for the last fortnight. I am writing this on the roadside during a ten minutes halt on a 36 mile march. I am still in the very best of health and hope you are the same. Give my love to Bertha and best wishes to yourself

I Remain your Sincerely
Alf

NEW ZEALANDERS SEATED UPON A CAPTURED ANTI-TANK GUN

FOR GOD AND THE EMPIRE
of Honour

ACKNOWLEDGEMENTS

The assistance of Creative New Zealand is gratefully acknowledged.

ROBYN BELTON would like to thank Richard Taylor, Elizabeth Cottrell, Christine Strachan of the QEII Army Memorial Museum, Waiouru; Annette Facer, Hocken Library, University of Otago; Brian Connor, Otago Military Museum; Otago Early Settlers' Museum, Dunedin; Alan Beckhuis, Alexander Turnbull Library; Eva Yocum, Museum of New Zealand; Sarjeant Gallery, Wanganui; Bishop Suter Art Gallery, Nelson; Hardwicke Knight Collection; National Archives of New Zealand; Tom Brooking and Paul Enright, historians, Dunedin; Jill Stuff and Derek Schulz; John Fitzgerald and Jane Hyde; Judy and Geoff Anderson; Peter, Simon and Daniel Belton; Vivienne Leachman; Kelly Isabella Nichol and Bessie, her bantam.

JENNIFER BECK would like to thank Lynne Hayward for original research.

BIBLIOGRAPHY

Adam-Smith, Patsy. *The Anzacs*. Australia: Thomas Nelson Ltd.

Bairnsfather, Captain Bruce. "The Bystanders" *Fragments from France*.

Benson, Sir Irving. *The Man with the Donkey*. Hodder & Stoughton, 1965.

Brooking, Tom. *Milestones*. New Zealand: Mills Publication, 1988.

Coombes, Rose E. *Before Endeavours Fade*.

The Countess of Liverpool's Gift Book. Christchurch: Whitcombe and Tombs Ltd, 1915.

Gilbert, Adrian. *World War I in Photographs*. London: Guild, 1986.

Hodgson, Pat. *Animals in War*. England: Wayland Publications, 1978.

Macdonald, Lyn. *The Roses of No Man's Land*. London: Michael Joseph, 1980.

McKenzie, D. and Lindsay Malcolm. *Boots, Belts, Rifle and Pack. A New Zealand Soldier at War, 1917–1919*. New Zealand: John McIndoe, 1992.

Mr Punch's History of the Great War. London: Cassell & Co., 1920.

Otago Cavalcade 1916–1920. Hardwicke Knight.

Phillips, Jock, Nicholas Boyack and E.P. Malone. *The Great Adventure: NZ Soldiers Describe the First World War*. Wellington: Port Nicholson Press, 1988.

Pugsley, Christopher. *ANZAC – The New Zealanders at Gallipoli*. Hodder & Stoughton, 1993.

Stewart, Col. H. *The NZ Division: Official History of New Zealand's Effort in the Great War*. Christchurch: Whitcombe and Tombs Ltd, 1921.

Tolerton, Jane. *Ettie: The Life of Ettie Rout*. Auckland: Penguin, 1992.